Mr. Kind uses lyrical rhyme coupled with marvelous graphic imagery.

This is the tale of the once pompous Bluff who steals fun only to be brought down by the virtuous message delivered via a cryptic stranger and the light words of an earth angel, thus allowing the children to play and laugh again.

These are the stories that last for generations.

———

Mr. Kind Stories are a YouthWide jubilation produced in association with Prove Nothing.

Written By: Mr. Kind
Visualized By: Zacc Pollitt @provenothing
Mrkindstories.com @mrkindstories
©2018, YouthWide

To Hudson

There once was a man
named Bluff
who thought himself great
at all stuff.

Bluff wore gold hair,
had a wondrous stare,
and ran about all day
making dares.

Bluff had five marbles
that he kept in a match-box:

A great gold match-box
that was tied to seal close
with red ribbon locks.

Bluff ran around town,
all day long and all night,
shouting and hooting
and trying to pick fights.

"I am much better than any,"
Bluff said,
"Much better than Timmy,
or Jimmy, or Fred.

Much better," said Bluff
and rolled on the ground.
Bluff laughed and chuckled
and waved his marbles
up high.

" *HAHAA*

HA

HA "

Bluff told the whole world
that no one would win.
Bluff laughed at each person who
tried to play him.

So Bluff went on laughing about
the things that he said,
when suddenly the sky turned pitch black
and the sea turned blood red.

The ground around began to rumble and quake
and just as Bluff began to frown
a crack went on cracking
straight through the ground.

Bluff looked down quickly to find a crack
that worked its way between his legs
from far in front to far past his back.
A thick purple haze seeped up from the crack.

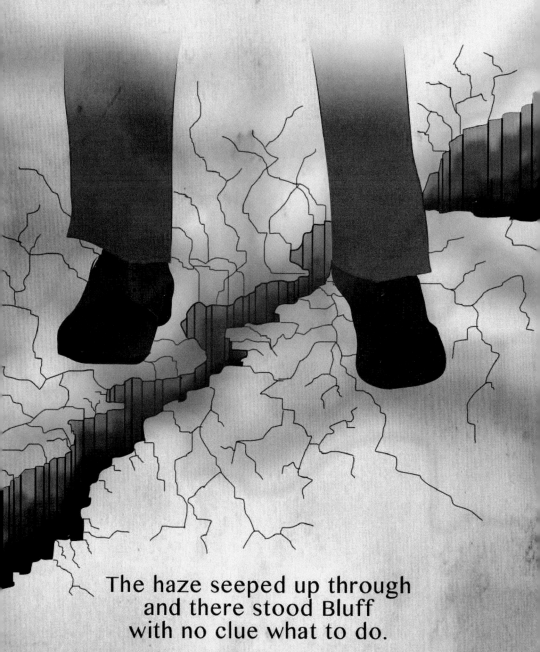

The haze seeped up through
and there stood Bluff
with no clue what to do.

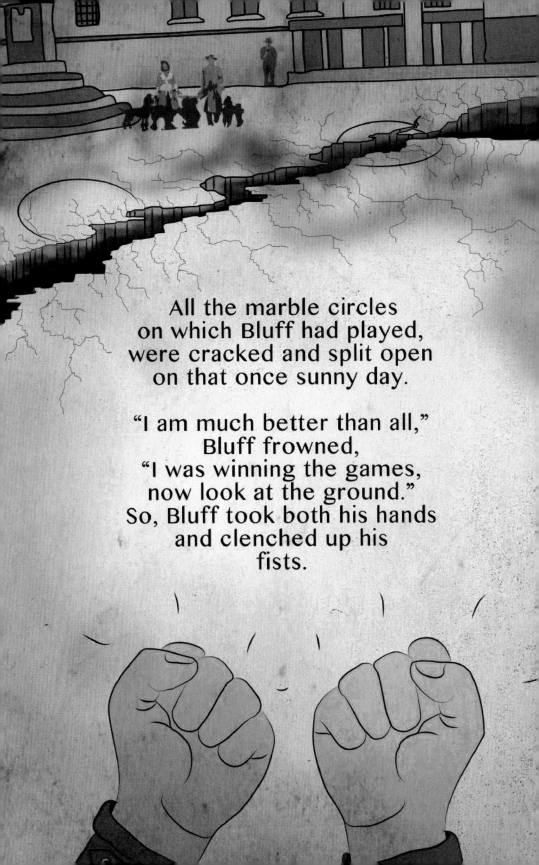

All the marble circles
on which Bluff had played,
were cracked and split open
on that once sunny day.

"I am much better than all,"
Bluff frowned,
"I was winning the games,
now look at the ground."
So, Bluff took both his hands
and clenched up his
fists.

"I demand to see," he cried,
"who has done this!"
And with that came a stranger
up through the haze

right from the ground:
A tall, straight arm stranger
wore a sun yellow suit,
a moon dusted vest,
and red leather boots.

The stranger so slowly worked his way up
through the purple stained mist,
stepped down right before Bluff and said,
"I am the one who has done this."

The yellow suited stranger
quite calmly put a hand on Bluff's arm.
"Forgive me dear fellow," he said,
"but there is cause for alarm.

You see, I live down beneath
your great marble game hall
and all the things that I've heard
I don't like them one bit at all.

I have heard all the things
that you have said or have done
and...

" FROM THIS GAME

YOU HAVE STOLEN

ALL OF THE FUN."

So I am here now to play one marble game;
to beat you and, in so doing, make you tame.

Now, one and all please come gather around,"
so said the stranger, while a large marble circle
was drawn in the ground.

The stranger did firmly tip on his cap,
then pull from his pocket
four marbles and a shooter, quite fat.

The stranger waited a moment
before he threw his marbles into the ring
and looked at loud Bluff,
with a bitter sweet gleam.

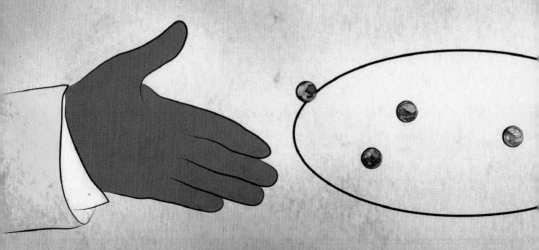

"Yes, yes well indeed," howled Bluff
somewhat steamed and held up
his gold match-box, four marbles,
and a shooter stained green.

"This is all quite silly," scowled Bluff
as he threw his four marbles into the ring,
"Quite silly indeed as I am the king!"

The stranger stood tall, right on top of the air,
showing a grin with a bitter cream stare.
So Bluff kneltdown sharply
and took the first shot.
Knocking out three marbles straight,
he sat down with a plop.

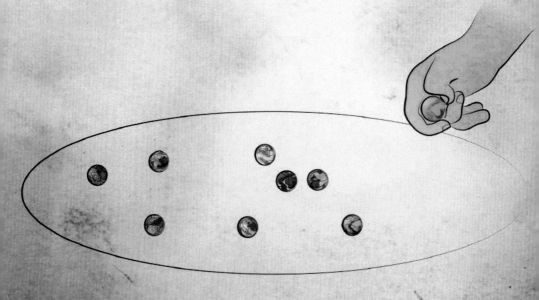

Bluff drew up a hand to his chin.
"Beat that Mr. Wonderful,"
he said with his grin.

"One shot," said the stranger,
"and I shall win."
So the stranger knelt down,
beside the marble game ring.
"One shot," hissed the stranger,
"and I will be king!"

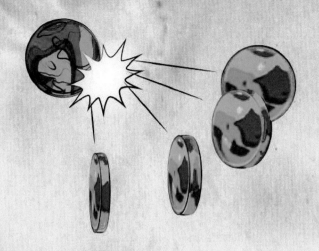

A great gasp of air
was heard around the floor
as the stranger hit the first marble...
which quickly split into four.

All the new marbles knocked out all the rest.
So, the stranger took a step back
and gently patted his chest,

then tipped on his cap,
as the only marble left
was the shooter, quite fat.

"Thank you, good people,"
the stranger began,
"You have all seen what you've seen
and big headed Bluff is no longer king."

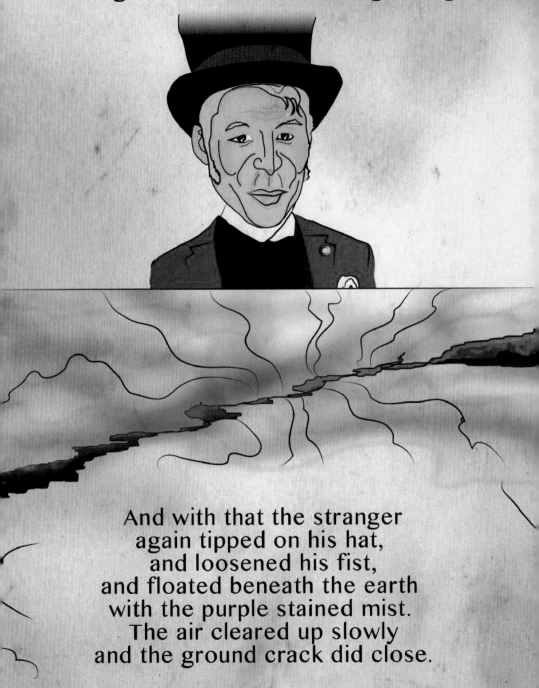

And with that the stranger
again tipped on his hat,
and loosened his fist,
and floated beneath the earth
with the purple stained mist.
The air cleared up slowly
and the ground crack did close.

Now all the children sat on the roof
and pointed at Bluff to call him a goof
as all the marble players who had never won
sat in a circle in the middle of town

and played one game of marbles,
one game just for fun.
Bluff sat in the dirt with no friends
and his face in his fists crying,

"My dear lord, oh lord,
what has done this?"
Bluff went on crying into his hands
when a dirt colored angel came on up
from the land.

She smelled like fudge brownies
from a baker's bowl
and on her cheek
she did carry
a purple stained mole.

She had no wings
and no wand of her own.
She moved toward Bluff
and began with a moan,
"Oh, my dear child
what have you done?

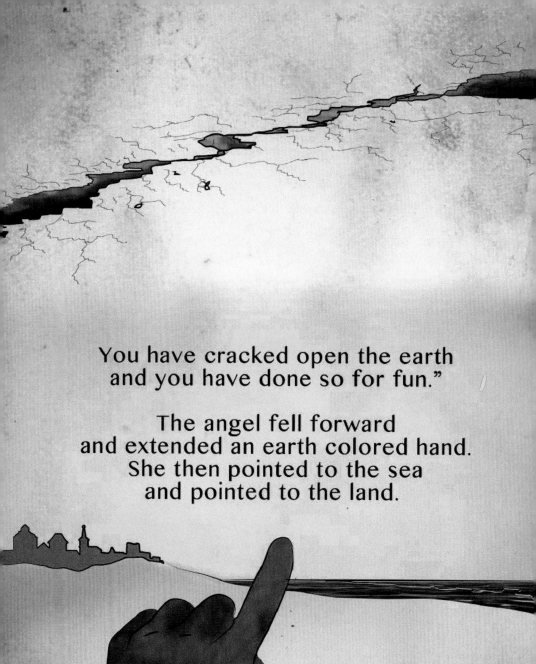

You have cracked open the earth
and you have done so for fun."

The angel fell forward
and extended an earth colored hand.
She then pointed to the sea
and pointed to the land.

"The message," spoke the angel,
"is quite clear.
Indeed," whispered the angel,
"it is my dear."
With that, the angel cupped Bluff's face,
leaned and spoke in a medium pace...

"NO MATTER HOW GRAND

YOU MAY THINK YOU ARE

THERE MAY BE SOMEONE MUCH BETTER

MUCH BETTER BY FAR."

THE END